detail
for not band stand-
3-1-05

New Collar

detail
page 32

additional

HIGH IN
THE CLOUDS

HIGH IN
THE CLOUDS

Paul McCartney,
Geoff Dunbar and Philip Ardagh

First published in 2005 by Faber and Faber Limited

3 Queen Square London WC1N 3AU

Typeset by Faber and Faber Limited

Printed in Belgium by Proost

Donna Payne, Designer • Tom Cook, Digital Artist • Suzy Jenvey, Editor

A CIP record for this book

is available from the British Library

ISBN 0-571-22501-2

2 4 6 8 10 9 7 5 3 1

PAUL MCCARTNEY's lifelong interest in children's storytelling grew out of his childhood love of classic Disney. He has created a number of animated films in collaboration with Geoff Dunbar, including *Rupert and the Frog Song*, which won a BAFTA for best animated short film and became the bestselling short video of the year. His recent animated releases have included *Daumier's Law*, which won a BAFTA for best short animated film, *Tropic Island Hum*, and *Tuesday*.

GEOFF DUNBAR is one of the world's finest animation directors. Among his many awards for film and television Geoff has received two BAFTAs, a Palme d'Or at Cannes, a Golden Bear at Berlin, a Grand Prix at Ottawa and La Spiga d'Ore at Valladolid. Geoff lives near Oxford, with his wife Jan and their five young children.

PHILIP ARDAGH has written over sixty children's books and is probably best known for his best-selling *Eddie Dickens* trilogy, currently translated into over 25 languages.

This book is dedicated to the ones we love

W irral the squirrel is lying back on his favourite branch, munching acorns from a bag as he listens to his mum telling one of her stories. It's like eating popcorn while you're enjoying a good film. This is one of Sugartail's Animalia tales, set on the tropical island sanctuary where the animals live without a care in the world.

Wirral smiles. Things aren't bad here either: a cool summer breeze, a good story and the crunchiest of crunchy snacks. Unlike life in Megatropolis. He glances over to the huge ugly cityscape on the horizon, shrouded in pollution.

Dotted among the branches of the trees, like notes on sheet music, sit the Woodland creatures, all captivated by Sugartail's words. All, that is, except for Snooze the owl, who's doing what he does best in the daytime: snoring gently. It's nothing personal. He's a night bird.

For as long as Wirral can remember, his mother,

Sugartail, has been the Woodland storyteller and, for as long as he can remember, he's loved the stories about Animalia best.

She's coming to the part of the story where the island animals are about to throw a big party for some reason or other (or for no reason at all), when Wirral feels the branch begin to vibrate.

It's just a tremble to begin with . . . but then the tremble becomes a shudder . . . and the shudder becomes a J-J-UDDDDDDER!!!

Tethered to its usual branch is a hot-air balloon, and in its wicker basket stands Froggo, a frog. (The clue is in the name.) He's a regular visitor to the Woodland, coming and going when the mood – and the wind – takes him. He may be green, furless and lack a tail, but Wirral thinks that he's a fun amphibian to be around.

No sooner has the tree started to shake than Froggo has fired up the balloon and is floating it above the treetops to see what's going on. He can't believe his froggy eyes. In fact, he takes off his glasses and gives both lenses a good clean on a corner of his scarf before putting them back on again, just to be doubly sure.

But things still look just as bad, in fact, more so. 'Bulldozers!' shouts Froggo. 'A whole battalion of them!'

And he's not lying.

What follows is a nightmare of noise and destruction. What the huge caterpillar tyres don't flatten is either pushed over, thrown aside or torn apart by the bulldozers and their merciless metal teeth. Petrol-powered chainsaws splutter to life, whining their way through tree trunk after tree trunk, slicing, slashing, killing the Woodland.

The animals flee in all directions, abandoning their homes and trees in a desperate bid to save themselves. Even Snooze is now as wide awake as he's ever been, and has taken flight.

Wirral dashes straight down the tree trunk, like only a squirrel can, looking back over his shoulder to make sure that Mum is close behind him.

She isn't.

Suddenly, the huge old tree is falling . . . falling . . . and, moments later, Sugartail's limp white body lies twisted beneath a broken branch. 'No!' cries Wirral. 'No!' He claws at the soft earth with his tiny paws and drags her out from under it.

His mother opens an eye and somehow manages to speak. 'You must go far from here,' she whispers. Wirral has to lean in close to hear her above the noise of the mayhem all around them. He can smell sweet chestnuts on her breath. 'You must find Animalia. You'll be safe there . . . It's a real island, Wirral . . . It's real . . .'

Which is how talk of this magical

sanctuary comes to be Sugartail's final words. Wirral gently lies her lifeless body on a patch of springy moss.

'Wirral! Hurry!' says a voice. 'Get in. We must leave. Now!'

The young squirrel turns to see Froggo hovering close by in his balloon, a rope ladder trailing from the basket to the ground.

Wirral shakes his head and says something Froggo can't hear above the deafening sound of the destruction all around them.

'It's too late for your dear mother!' Froggo shouts. 'You must save yourself.'

'There's something I must do first,' Wirral calls up. 'Alone.'

*   *   *

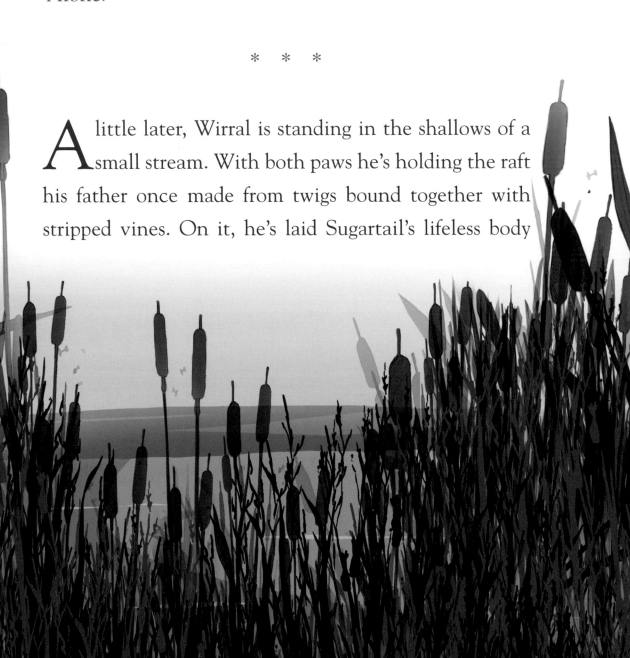

A little later, Wirral is standing in the shallows of a small stream. With both paws he's holding the raft his father once made from twigs bound together with stripped vines. On it, he's laid Sugartail's lifeless body and has covered it with every type of wild flower he could find in the chaos.

'Goodbye, Mum,' he whispers, and he lets go of the raft which is instantly caught by the current and carried swiftly downstream, away from the terrifying events in what's left of her beloved Woodland. At a respectful distance, a few of the animals, braving the dangers of the bulldozers and chainsaws, look on.

Wirral only turns from the stream when the raft is fully out of sight. Froggo strides towards him. Though one of his legs is wooden, he moves with surprising

speed. 'Now will you come with me?' he pleads.

'I need to do some thinking,' says Wirral, head bent low. There's an ear-splitting creak and a tree comes crashing down only inches away from him. He doesn't even seem to notice.

Froggo sighs a wide-mouthed sigh and reaches inside the pocket of his flying jacket. He pulls out a small blue envelope and presses it into Wirral's paw. 'I understand,' he says, 'but there's something *you* need to understand, Wirral. If you ever need me, open that, follow the instructions and I'll be there. Okay?'

'Okay,' says Wirral. 'Thank you.' His mind is clearly on other things. Well, one thing in fact: trying to find the island of Animalia.

*   *   *

With the Woodland in its dying moments and his friends all gone, Wirral decides to look for answers in the city. Thrusting a few hastily snatched items into a rucksack, he begins his long trek. The squirrel isn't aware of time. He doesn't keep track of how many days it takes him to reach Megatropolis. Two? Three? All he knows is that his old life is over and that his feet are very sore.

When he finally arrives at the sprawling outskirts of the
city, it comes as a surprise. From the treetops of the
Woodland, Megatropolis looked to be made up almost
entirely of skyscrapers. Here in front of him, though, is a
shanty town of cardboard boxes and packing crates. The

word STYX has been crudely painted onto a makeshift
sign made out of an old plank. Wirral wrinkles his nose.
This neighbourhood smells bad.

Picking his way through the rubbish and past the
shacks, he sees Styx's inhabitants watching him with

dull eyes. Although he sees animals of many different kinds, they all have much in common: they look hungry, dirty and desperate. It's with a real sense of relief that Wirral finally comes to a road and sees proper brick-built houses beyond. Stepping off the pavement, there's a terrible *'ROAAAAARRRRR!'* as a huge automobile thunders straight towards him.

The squirrel finds himself flying through the air as, at the very last moment, he's yanked to safety by a pair of strong paws.

* * *

'Thanks for saving my skin,' Wirral splutters, struggling to his feet and dusting himself down. He has the foul taste of the car's exhaust fumes in his mouth. 'I'm William the Squirrel but my friends call me Wirral.'

'Hi, Wirral,' says the creature – a young rat – who's undoubtedly just saved his life. 'I'm Ratsy. You may have

heard of my dad, Papa Ratsy?' He pauses and grins, then
adds: 'The photographer?'

Wirral shakes his head. 'No. Sorry. I'm from out
of town.'

'Never mind,' says Ratsy with a shake of the head. 'I
should have guessed that from your road sense.'

'My what?'

'Exactly. You don't have none.' Ratsy tilts back his
head and sniffs the air. 'Need someone with a nose for
the city to show you around?' he asks.

'You'd do that for me?' asks Wirral.

'Sure I would,' says Ratsy, grinning another ratty grin. 'Squirrels are just tree rats, ain't they? That makes you a kinda country cousin. We're as good as related!' He takes his baseball hat off his own head and plonks it down on top of Wirral's. He then slaps the squirrel on the back, almost sending him stumbling back out into the path of the on-coming traffic.

Despite everything that has happened to him, Wirral actually finds himself smiling for the first time in days. Perhaps Megatropolis won't be so bad after all, he thinks. Not with a friend like Ratsy around.

We live and learn.

* * *

Ratsy has work to do, apparently, but arranges to meet up with Wirral later.

'When you hear the evening-shift siren sound, come to the Chow Down,' he says.

'How will I hear the evening-shift siren . . . or recognise it?' asks Wirral. 'And where is the Chow Down?'

Ratsy grins another one of his sharp-toothed ratty grins. 'Don't worry, you'll hear the siren all right, and when you do, you'll know it. As for the Chow Down, it's the building shaped like a big bowl.' He points into the distance.

Before Wirral knows quite what's happening, Ratsy dashes off with a 'See you later!', disappearing down an alleyway.

'Er, b-bye!' Wirral shouts after him.

Not knowing quite how much time he has to kill before they meet again – if Ratsy really does show up, that is – Wirral decides to explore the city, keeping the Chow Down in view.

After a while, he catches sight of a very rare thing in Megatropolis. It's a tree! And, because squirrels and trees go together like dogs and lampposts (or hippos and mud-baths), Wirral heads for it. It's as he rounds the corner that he first lays eyes on Wilhamina. She's a beautiful young red squirrel . . . and is being bothered by a couple of badgers.

'I said, leave me alone!' says Wilhamina bravely, her voice trembling ever-so-slightly.

'Or what?' snarls the bigger of the badgers. 'You'll

tickle us with that big bushy tail of yours?'

'Ooooo! I'm *so* scared!' taunts the other.

Wirral's got to do something . . . but what use is one more squirrel against two mean-looking badgers? Everyone knows that they're all muscle! He dashes up the trunk of the tree behind them, and into the branches. From his squirrel's-eye vantage point he looks down. 'Leave the kid alone!' he shouts, trying to make his voice sound as deep and threatening as possible.

'Or what?' repeats the bigger badger.

By way of an answer, Wirral drops his rucksack between the branches straight onto the bully's head. 'Or the rest of us will come and get you!' he yells.

Rubbing his head, the bigger badger stares up through the leaves with a slightly dazed expression, trying to see just how many other squirrels there really are up there. Wilhamina seizes the opportunity to dash up the tree herself.

'Now clear off!' shouts Wirral.

Snatching the rucksack, the badgers do just that, fearing attack from a squirrel army!

Up in the leafy branches, Wilhamina turns to Wirral. 'Thanks for coming to my rescue,' she says. 'I would have been fine, but you speeded things up a little . . . and I'm sorry about your losing your stuff.'

'That's okay,' says Wirral. They swap names. It's good to be talking to another squirrel again. 'Megatropolis seems such a horrible place,' he says. 'I've only been here a few hours, and I've almost been run over, and now this!'

'You haven't even scratched the surface,' says Wilhamina. She scampers out to the end of a branch and points to a skylight on the roof of a vast building sprawled out beneath them.

Wirral finds himself looking through the glass into an enormous factory, filled with animal workers, each with that same look of hopelessness he's seen back in the Styx.

Up on a ledge, high above the factory floor stands

the biggest, fattest rat Wirral has ever laid eyes on. The
buttons on his waistcoat are set to burst.

'That's Wackford, the boss's right-hand rat,' says
Wilhamina. 'Foreman of all her factories. Her Mr Fixit.'

At that moment, Wackford cracks an evil-looking

whip. 'Get on with it, you lazy layabouts!' he bellows. 'There are orders to be filled! Productivity targets to be met!'

It's then that Wirral notices a huge 'G' logo on the factory wall. There's something frighteningly familiar about it.

'It's slave labour,' Wilhamina explains. 'The poor animals in the Styx work to make the city dwellers even richer. The very poorest of them never even get to leave the factories at all. They're prisoners.'

'If only we could get everyone to Animalia,' Wirral mutters, the rage growing inside him.

'You know about the island?' asks Wilhamina in amazement. 'I have a friend who's heard stories about –'

Just then, there's a terrible CRUNCH . . . Froggo has crash-landed his hot-air balloon in the tree!

'Hello! Hello!' grins Wirral's froggy friend. 'Sorry I'm late.'

'Late?' says Wirral. 'But I didn't know you were coming.'

'I was talking to Wilhamina,' says his amphibian pal. Then his face breaks into another toothless smile. 'Wirral! It's you! I didn't recognise you in that cap. How good to see you again so soon!'

'You know Froggo?' Wirral asks Wilhamina just as Wilhamina asks him exactly the same question.

Wilhamina tells Froggo how Wirral rescued her from the badgers.

'This part of the city isn't the safest place to be,' says Froggo, 'which is why I'm going to give young Wilhamina here a ride home.'

'Why not come to the Chow Down to meet Ratsy?' Wirral says excitedly.

'When?' asks Wilhamina.

'When the evening-shift siren sounds,' says Wirral. 'Whenever that –' His words are drowned out by a sound so loud that it buffets the hot-air balloon against the branches and makes Wirral and Wilhamina's fur blow out in one direction, as though they're standing by a giant hairdryer. To say that the noise is loud would be like saying that the Grand Canyon is 'a bit of a crack in the ground'.

When it finally stops, Wirral's ears are ringing and he's sh-sh-shaking. 'Th-th-that was the e-e-evening-shift s-s-siren, w-w-wasn't it?'

'Yup-p-p,' says W-W-Wilhamina.

'It most certainly w-w-was,' nods F-F-Froggo. 'Now

the evening shift will start in all the factories across
the c-c-city.'

*   *   *

Froggo gives them a lift to the Chow Down. Wirral
has never seen so many animals crowded together.
He's used to the wide-open spaces of the Woodland . . .
which is, of course, no more.

Ratsy, however, seems totally at home. 'Hi,' he says cheerily as he wanders in through the door. 'I sees you got us a good table. Now, let's eat!'

The food arrives and they talk. Ratsy tells them more about himself.

'I work for the most powerful player in Megatropolis,'

he says proudly. 'Her name's Gretsch. If you ain't heard of her yet, you soon will. She owns all the factories round here.'

'She pretty much runs the city,' Wilhamina adds.

Wirral thinks of the 'G' logo on the bulldozers and in the factory. G for Gretsch? he wonders. More than likely. 'Don't you hate working for someone who treats other animals so badly?' he asks.

The young rat shrugs. 'That's just how it is,' he says. 'Rich and poor. Free and slaves. It's always been that way.'

'Not everywhere,' says Wirral. 'In the Woodland we were free . . . until now.' He pauses. 'But in Animalia, all the animals are free, equal and safe.'

'Where?' asks Ratsy, and Wirral tells him about the amazing island. 'Wow!' says Ratsy, when he's finished. 'It sounds a cool place, but are you sure it ain't just make-believe?'

'It's real,' says Wirral, remembering his mother's final words.

'Want to see where Gretsch lives?' asks Ratsy, once they've finished eating. (His treat.) 'It's an amazing apartment and I know a secret way in!'

'What about one of her factories?' suggests Wirral, an idea forming in his mind. He's already considering a great escape!

Ratsy shakes his head. 'No way,' he says. 'All the locks on all the gates of all the factories are computer-controlled, and only Gretsch knows the password.'

'Then let's see her apartment,' says Wirral.

In the shadows stands an eavesdropper: a certain large and very frightening rat, with buttons set to burst. 'Animalia, huh?' he grins. 'How very interesting.'

Ratsy leads the two young squirrels through a warren of passages beneath the city: sewers, long-forgotten service tunnels, a disused railway tunnel, rainwater outlets and vast pipes of every description. There is a constant drip-drip-dripping, the air is dank and, more often than not, the walls are very slimy. After a while they reach an underground river.

'We must cross here!' says Ratsy, his voice echoing.

'How?' asks Wirral. 'Stilts?'

'Gladys!' grins Ratsy.

'What's a gladys?' asks Wilhamina.

'Gladys isn't a *what*, she's a *who*!' explains Ratsy. He lets out a piercing whistle and the head of an enormous crocodile breaks through the surface of the water. The squirrels rear back in surprise.

The croc smiles. She appears to have no teeth at all. Not one. 'Oh, hello –' She pauses.

'Ratsy,' says Ratsy.

'Ah, yes, Ratsy,' nods Gladys the crocodile. 'Forgive me, my eyesight isn't what it used to be, and all you

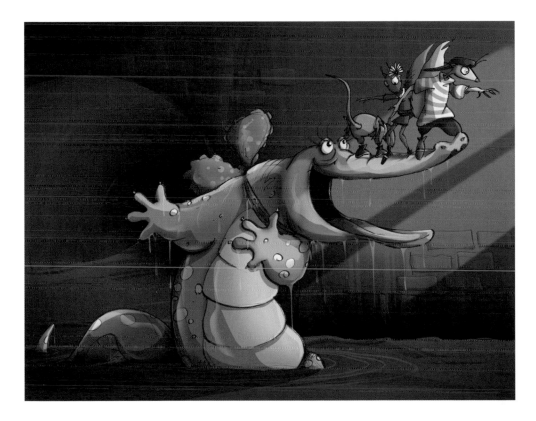

sewer rats do look much the same to me.'

'We was hopin' for a ride across the river, Gladys,' says Ratsy, ignoring the sewer-rat comment, though – even in this dim light – Wirral can see that he didn't like it!

'I'd be happy to oblige!' says the crocodile. 'Do, please, climb aboard.'

Her long snout acts like a swing bridge. They step onto her nose on one side of the river, she swings it

33

across and they step off onto the other.

'Thank you!' Wirral calls out. 'Thank you so much!'

'My pleasure,' beams Gladys. 'I'm most glad of the company. I'm an opera singer, you see! The acoustics down here are splendid. Do come again!' Then she bursts into song: *'Come again my rodent friends! Down the pipes and round the bends . . .* I write all my own material, you know.'

* * *

At long last, Wirral, Wilhamina and Ratsy reach an enormous service duct, full of brightly-coloured pipes rising high above them like multicoloured columns, some painted with polka dots and others stripy like barber's poles.

'These lead up to Gretsch's pad,' says Ratsy. 'Even her plumbing's got style!' he adds, with a hint of pride. 'Real designer stuff.'

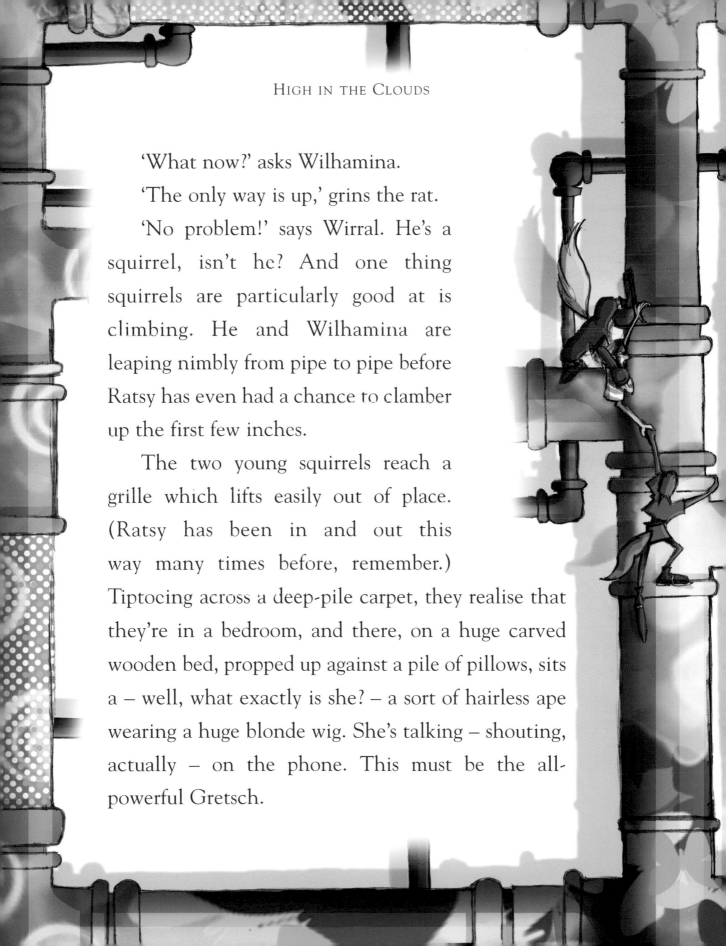

'What now?' asks Wilhamina.

'The only way is up,' grins the rat.

'No problem!' says Wirral. He's a squirrel, isn't he? And one thing squirrels are particularly good at is climbing. He and Wilhamina are leaping nimbly from pipe to pipe before Ratsy has even had a chance to clamber up the first few inches.

The two young squirrels reach a grille which lifts easily out of place. (Ratsy has been in and out this way many times before, remember.) Tiptoeing across a deep-pile carpet, they realise that they're in a bedroom, and there, on a huge carved wooden bed, propped up against a pile of pillows, sits a – well, what exactly is she? – a sort of hairless ape wearing a huge blonde wig. She's talking – shouting, actually – on the phone. This must be the all-powerful Gretsch.

She doesn't look particularly stylish to me, thinks Wirral.

'They said *what?*' Gretsch is demanding. 'Animalia? . . . Hmmm . . . Hmmm . . . Well, if it does exist then we must find it, Wackford!' she bellows into the phone, her wig wobbling with each shouted syllable.

The blood drains from Wirral's face. She's found out about the island! But how? When Gretsch speaks again, the terrible truth dawns on him.

'What else did this young squirrel have to say about the place?' she asks. Wackford speaks at the other end of the line. Gretsch listens, then issues her orders: 'We find Animalia and we *destroy* Animalia,' she proclaims. 'We can't let stories of a tropical island paradise spread. Symbols of hope must be eliminated . . .'

Wirral is stunned. He's been in Megatropolis less than a day and he's already put Animalia and its inhabitants in danger. This isn't how it's supposed to be!

He and Wilhamina are creeping past the ugly footboard of the enormous bed when Gretsch catches

sight of them. 'What have we here?' she snarls and, with frightening agility, she leaps from the bed to the floor. 'Wackford warned me to expect uninvited company!' she cries, in hot pursuit. 'Where's Ratsy, that treacherous little rat friend of yours?!' She makes a swipe for the young squirrels and – horror of horrors – manages to get Wilhamina in her claw-like grip, her wig falling askew.

'GOTCHA!' she snarls, in triumph.

Wirral spins around and starts running to the aid of his captured friend. Everything is going wrong, so terribly wrong!

'NO!' Wilhamina cries. 'Find Animalia! Warn the animals!'

'But –'

'Just GO!' Wilhamina shouts.

'I – I'll be back!' cries Wirral. In his heart of hearts, he knows that he's defenceless against whatever kind of creature this Gretsch is. He dives through the grille opening and darts back down the coloured pipes to safety. There's no sign of Ratsy anywhere, and Wirral will need help to rescue Wilhamina and to find the island. Luckily, he knows just the right animal to do that: Froggo! He's even got his own transport.

Running through the endless maze of tunnels, Wirral heads for a spot of daylight and finds another way out, through luck more than anything. Back in the fresh air at last, he digs his hand in his pocket and pulls out the small blue envelope that Froggo gave him back in the Woodland. It's a little crumpled, but none the worse for wear. He tears it open. Inside is a blue card on which is written: 'Light blue touch paper and retire.'

Wirral frowns. That's what it says on fireworks, he recalls, remembering an impressive display Froggo put on in the Woodland one year. How strange. The young squirrel lights the card using a book of matches from the Chow Down.

The card shoots up into the air and explodes into an awe-inspiring and can-it-really-be-happening fireworks display of utter brilliance with showers of sparks, bangs,

flares and spangles – which ends with the sky being filled with the word FROGGO. These then fall away, letter by letter, like fairy dust.

'Wow! That was impossible . . .' Wirral muses, which is something of an understatement. 'Now what?'

Less than five minutes have passed when Wirral spots a tiny dot in the sky. It gets bigger and bigger as it gets nearer and nearer. It's Froggo's balloon and it's coming this w-w-w-waaaaaaaaaaaay!

'LOOK OUT!' shouts Wirral, as the large wicker basket comes to earth with a thud, missing him by a squirrel's whisker (if squirrels have whiskers).

With no time to lose, Wirral clambers aboard, telling the amphibious aviator of Wilhamina's capture and his need to find Animalia.

'We must rescue Wilhamina and warn the islanders of Gretsch's plan,' says Wirral. 'It's my fault she found out about it in the first place!'

'No, we must warn the islanders first and *then* enlist their help to rescue Wilhamina and all the enslaved animals. That's the way to do it!' says Froggo. 'Now, where exactly is it?'

'Where's what?'

'Animalia.'

'I don't know,' Wirral confesses.

'Your mother never told you how to get there?'

'No.'

'Oh,' says Froggo looking about as crestfallen as a crestfallen frog can look. 'Never mind. The thing about islands is that they're all surrounded by water, so let's begin by searching the seven seas.'

'All seven?' sighs Wirral. 'Where should we start?'

Froggo grins another froggy grin. 'We'll let the balloon decide.'

* * *

Time passes. Winds change. Clear blue skies become dark and brooding. Wirral and Froggo are in the middle of a storm. Waves crash below them while thunder crashes above. A fork of lightning tickles the edge of the basket.

'That was too close for comfort!' cries Froggo but he looks like he's loving every minute of it. Wirral, however, manages to look both airsick and seasick at the same time, and his grey fur is soaked right through . . .

Far away, back in Megatropolis, Wilhamina is in one of Gretsch's factories. To be more precise, she's in a cage in the basement in one of the factories. It's a bit like a dungeon and is where the day-shift workers are locked away at night for a few meagre hours of sleep. Daylight comes from one tiny barred glassless window, high up in the wall behind Wilhamina. She watches drops of rain trickle down the brickwork, hoping and praying that Wirral will get to warn the animals of Animalia in time.

'Hurry back,' she whispers with a shudder.

* * *

After two days and two nights, the storm clears and the white fluffy cotton-wool clouds part beneath Froggo's balloon to reveal a glorious tropical island shimmering in a sparkling sea. Great blue whales are leaping out of the ocean, as if to greet the newcomers.

'Is th-th-at . . . ?' Wirral stutters.

'It looks that way,' nods Froggo.

'But how . . . ?'

'Serendipity,' suggests Froggo.

'Seren-*what?*' asks Wirral.

'Dipity,' says Froggo. 'Fortuitous luck.'

'Magic, more like,' says Wirral in wonder.

After some tricky manoeuvring, the balloon finally touches down on the sun-warmed golden sands. Wirral and Froggo have been spotted, and a welcoming committee is waiting to greet the new arrivals: a single shaggy figure, towering high above them.

'Welcome to our island,' says the dapperly-dressed beast, his voice rich and deep like chocolate, with the hint of a chuckle. 'I am Chief Bison.'

'I'm Wirral and this is Froggo,' says the squirrel,

eager to get the introductions out of the way. 'We came to warn –'

'Greetings, Wirral. Greetings, Froggy,' says the chief as he removes his hat and makes a sweeping bow.

'It's Frog*go*, actually,' Froggo mutters, but Wirral is already urgently explaining why they've come, warning the chief of the dangers of Gretsch.

'You must prepare to defend yourselves!' he finishes.

Whatever reaction Wirral is expecting, it isn't this. Chief Bison lets out a rumbling *laugh*. 'We're quite safe here,' he says. 'Our island has always been free.'

Froggo and Wirral do their best to convince him otherwise. They jump up and down, they wave their arms around, and they tell the chief more about the evil Gretsch and her dreadful factories.

A frown appears on Chief Bison's shaggy great features. He puts his massive arms around Froggo and Wirral and guides them towards the lush green undergrowth. 'We must gather the council,' he announces gravely.

The meeting takes place in a clearing and is attended by all creatures great and small. Every single islander is given the chance to have his or her say, from the biggest elephant down to the smallest of beetles.

Chief Bison calls the meeting to order, and turns to Wirral. 'Now, please tell everybody what you told me about this hairless ape and her despicable plans,' he booms.

After listening to Wirral's sorry

tale there's much squawking, gibbering, grunting and general ballyhoo from the assembled company. Finally, after much discussion, it is agreed that the threat is real and that Animalia must be defended at all costs. 'After which we will free our imprisoned brothers and sisters from Megatropolis!' Chief Bison proclaims.

'Froggy here will fly back to the city and spread the news.'

'Actually, it's Froggo,' says the frog. 'Frog*go*. Short for Frogmorton. F–r–o–'

'And he'll need a map,' Wirral interrupts. 'We've no idea how we got here!'

'All in good time,' says Chief Bison. 'But first we must celebrate your arrival! Two honoured guests who risked life and limb' – he stares at Froggo's wooden leg – 'to warn us.'

The truth be told, Wirral and Froggo would be happier if preparations for defending the island got underway immediately, but Chief Bison won't hear a word of it. He's keen on island tradition.

'And the arrival of guests calls for what we call a tropic island hum,' he beams.

The hum is a musical celebration, and this particular hum goes on late into the night. Wirral wanders away from the centre of the celebrations and sits at the ocean's edge. He looks at the beautiful inky sky above, lit with glittering stars, and sees it mirrored by the silvery starfish swimming happily in the sea below. If only his mother,

Sugartail, had lived to see this . . . and if only Wilhamina was here to share it with him too.

*   *   *

Time passes. Back in Megatropolis, back in the basement dungeon of one of Gretsch's factories, back in her cage, Wilhamina is examining the bars of her prison. Through them, she can see a big bunch of keys hanging next to the television monitors at the guards' station.

'Trouble is, I need to get out of the cage to get to the key to get me out of the cage in the first place!' she sighs.

Suddenly, she gets a terrible itch in her tail and is about to give it a good scratch with her paws when a tiny voice shouts 'PLEASE BE CAREFUL WHERE YOU PUT YOUR CLAWS! I'M A CIRCUS FLEA IN SEARCH OF SOME WARM DRY FUR TO SPEND THIS COLD, WET NIGHT.' He hops into view. 'I'M ALFREDO,' says the flea.

'You're very large for a flea!' says Wilhamina in surprise.

'I work out,' says Alfredo modestly. He flexes his muscles.

Wilhamina introduces herself, and tells Alfredo how she ended up here. Like just about every other creature in Megatropolis, Alfredo seems to have one-hundred-and-one reasons of his own for hating Gretsch too. He hops over to the guards' station and tries to lift the keys . . . but they're a large bunch and he's only a

small flea. No luck. 'Sorry,' he says, exhausted after all that wasted effort.

Just then a very friendly, very green face appears at the tiny barred window high up in the wall.

'Froggo!' Wilhamina whoops.

'I thought I might find you here,' Froggo grins, holding on to the bars to steady his balloon. 'I think it's

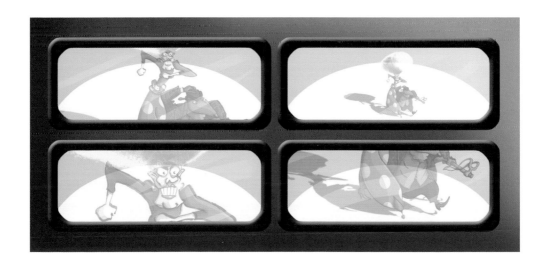

time I got you free. The animals of Animalia have been warned and –'

'AND HURRY!!!' squeaks Alfredo.

'Who said that?' asks a surprised Froggo, wondering whether the squirrel has an invisible friend.

'There's no time to explain,' says Wilhamina. She points at the keys on the bunch. 'One of those opens this.' She rattles the padlock to her cage.

'No problem,' says Froggo. He takes one of the guide ropes hanging from the basket of his balloon, leans through the bars, and in one – or two – fell swoops, he's lassoed the bunch of keys and flicked it over to Wilhamina, who frantically tries each key in the lock.

'HURRY!!!' Alfredo squeaks, even more urgently than before, as he sees Gretsch and Wackford on the monitors, getting closer and closer. 'GRETSCH AND WACKFORD ARE ON THEIR WAY!'

Bingo! Fourth key lucky. It turns in the lock and the squirrel spills out of her cage. She's free.

'This way!' Froggo urges, and Wilhamina scrambles

up the guide rope still dangling from the tiny window.

'What about freeing the others from the factory?' she pants.

'YOU GO!' shouts Alfredo. 'LEAVE IT TO THE FLEA! I'LL TRY TO SET THEM FREE!'

Oh, it's a *flea*, Froggo smiles to himself. No wonder I can't see him from here!'

'I'M GOOD WITH COMPUTERS!' Alfredo shouts. 'I'LL TRY TO FIND GRETSCH'S PASSWORD TO OPEN ALL THE DOORS AND GATES!'

Gretsch and Wackford burst into the room just in time to see Wilhamina scrambling through the window into the basket of Froggo's balloon.

'Quick! They're getting away!' screams Gretsch. She's quivering with rage, her wig wobbling like a giant trifle.

Wackford simply smiles, whips out an extraordinary-looking device – half gun, half catapult – and fires it at the balloon.

'Missed!' shouts Froggo, as the balloon takes flight.

'Not exactly,' grins Wackford. He turns to Gretsch. 'They'll never know it's there,' he says.

But what the evil rat and his even-more-evil mistress Gretsch don't know is that there's a highly intelligent flea sitting quietly on the computer keyboard.

As Froggo and Wilhamina sail off through the clouds towards Animalia, laughing in triumph and relief at her dramatic rescue, Gretsch and Wackford hurry this way and that, down various corridors and through various heavily-guarded doorways, until they reach one huge riveted iron door.

Gretsch punches in a code and the door opens to reveal her very own state-of-the-art custom-built gunboat! They clamber aboard and are soon seated on the bridge.

Wackford flicks a few switches and a map of the ocean appears on a screen. There's a flashing dot of light. 'There they are,' grins the *rattus rattus*. 'Now all we have to do is follow them.'

It wasn't Wilhamina or Froggo he'd been firing at back in the basement, but Froggo's balloon. And it wasn't a bullet he'd fired but an electronic tracking device . . . now firmly embedded in the base of the wicker basket, which Gretsch will be able to trace all the way to Animalia.

'Victory is in my grasp!' she cackles, her wig wobbling again, this time with excitement.

Alfredo, meanwhile, is hard at work at the computer keyboard, trying to find a way to access Gretsch's secret password. He jumps from key to key, grunting at the effort and muttering 'Oh dear, oh dear, oh dear'. Every time he presses 'Enter' the words . . .

ACCESS DENIED

. . . appear, taunting him on the screen. But he isn't about to give up.

* * *

With the map Chief Bison gave him, and his own remarkable knowledge of air currents, slipstreams and all things aeronautical, it takes less than a day for Froggo to steer his balloon back to Animalia.

It's Rumpus, the monkey on lookout duty up a palm tree, who's the first to spot the dot in the sky. 'Company! We've got company!' he jabbers.

'Friend or foe?' asks Chief Bison, woken from a nap. He slips on his jacket.

'Can't tell! Can't tell!' chatters Rumpus.

'Friends!' says Caw-Caw, a brightly-coloured parrot swooping in to land on the chief's shoulder. 'It's Froggo and he's got a red squirrel with him!'

'That'll be Wilhamina!' says an excited Wirral. He and the islanders swarm around the balloon as it comes in to land.

'Mission accomplished, I see!' Chief Bison gives a deep, throaty chuckle. 'Well done, Froggy!'

'It's Frogg*o*, with an "o", actually –' says the frog,

climbing from the basket, but his words are drowned out by the cheers of the other animals as they scoop the returning hero up onto Chief Bison's shoulder.

Wilhamina throws her arms around Wirral and gives him the greatest hug of his life, when . . . CRACK! There's an explosion. Someone's firing at the island!

WOMPF! Now mortar shells are exploding all around them. CRUMPH! The animal islanders scatter in all directions. A palm tree is split in two and comes crashing to the ground. Gretsch's gunboat is announcing her arrival!

'To the defences!' orders Chief Bison, and what feeble defences they turn out to be. Animalia is an island that's only ever known peace. The animals seem to know nothing about warfare. They have a single barricade ringing the island, made up of wooden boxes, carts – some even still have fruit in them – driftwood, some fencing and even an old mangle that was washed up from a sinking cargo ship in 1896.

And the islanders' weapons? Broom handles, branches, saucepans, ladles and piles of coconuts, some of which an enraged Rumpus the monkey is lobbing in the direction of the gunboat. They all fall short of their target, landing with useless thuds in the wet sand of the shoreline.

A baby hippo (called Muddles) has somehow managed to find a pair of boxing gloves, and is punching the air, grunting with the effort of each jab.

The only animals with any real protection are the armadillo with his scales and a very very old tortoise with his shell – neither of which is a defence against bullets and mortars.

But every animal stands shoulder to shoulder to defend their island and the freedom it stands for. Wirral and Wilhamina run to join this brave ragbag army and, between them, they hold the flag of Animalia up high.

'FREEDOM!' shout the islanders, waving what so-called weapons they have.

A voice cuts through the air, blasted through speakers on the gunboat: *'Surrender and I'll spare you for my factories!'* Wirral instantly recognises it as Gretsch herself. *'FIGHT, AND I'LL TAKE NO PRISONERS!'*

On board, Wackford is doing what he does best: giving orders. 'Reload the guns!' he barks. And who's the only other crew member on board? Who's that staggering across the floor with a huge mortar shell in his paws? It's none other than Ratsy, the first so-called friend Wirral made on arriving in Megatropolis!

'Aye, Aye, cap'n,' he says, loading the enormous gun.

Soon another deadly round of shells is fired, hitting the barricade but, fortunately, none of the animals. The islanders quickly scurry around repairing the break, the birds hauling pieces into place with their beaks, what little good it'll do them. If ever the phrase 'fighting a losing battle' seems right, it seems right right now!

But things are about to change. Suddenly, the gunboat starts listing, tilting first one way and then the other. Wackford loses his footing and falls with a thud. Gretsch slams into a wall – her face pressing up flat against a porthole – but manages to stay upright, which is more than can be said for her wig, which now has a jaunty leaning-tower-of-Pisa look about it.

'What's happening?' she screams.

What's happening is that Gretsch hasn't bargained for Animalia's sea defences. With all her thoughts on destroying the island itself, it hadn't occurred to her that the real threat may lie in the water. And now a small fleet of whales rises to the surface. Peace-loving,

beautiful and graceful whales may be, but they're also mighty BIG. They swim round and round the gunboat, causing it to bob about like a plastic duck in a bath.

Up in the balloon, piloted by Froggo, Chief Bison throws a huge net over the gunboat. (It's a net which Wirral last saw strung up between the trees, covered in balloons, and used as a roof for the band during the tropic island hum!)

The whales grab the edges of the net in their mouths, holding the gunboat like a fly in a spider's web. A mighty cheer goes up from the animals on the barricade on the shore.

'Surrender!' Chief Bison bellows, through a home-made megaphone.

Gretsch comes out onto the deck and looks up at him through the meshing of the net. 'Or you'll do what?' she laughs.

The net still clenched firmly in their mouths, the whales turn and begin to swim away from the boat in different directions. The net tightens, beginning to push the gunboat beneath the surface.

Froggo is whispering in the bison's ear. The chief nods, then speaks to Gretsch again: 'Tell us the password that opens the gates to all your evil factories. All your slaves and prisoners must be freed.'

'Never!' screams Gretsch. 'I've fought tougher animals than you!'

'Wait!' someone cries, above the din.

Back on the shore, Wirral turns to Wilhamina. 'I know that voice. It's Ratsy!'

'Traitor!' cries Wilhamina.

Now Ratsy can be seen on deck. 'Wait!' he repeats. 'The password is –' Wackford bursts through a doorway and chases the smaller rat, who's dodging this way and that. 'INCARCERATE! It's INCARCERATE!' With that, Ratsy dives off the edge of the boat, leaving Wackford clutching thin air.

Another cheer goes up from the Animalian islanders. The whales use the net to drag the boat ashore, beaching it on the golden sands. The animals throw their hats in the air in celebration. Well, not just their hats. Anything, in fact . . . including each other! Rumpus grabs Muddles the little hippo's arm and holds it up, like a referee declaring the winner of a boxing bout. Caw-Caw the parrot wheels and dives through the sky above them, performing victory roll after victory roll.

'Not bad for your first battle,' Froggo tells the bison as they come in to land.

'And hopefully our last, Froggo,' says the chief.

'Actually it's Froggy,' says Froggo and then stops himself. He grins a froggy grin and then laughs out loud. 'No, you were right the first time!'

Chief Bison, meanwhile, is off wading into the water. He drags out a very bedraggled and crestfallen looking Ratsy indeed.

Wirral and Wilhamina run over to the young rat. 'Were you on Gretsch's side all along?' Wirral demands. 'Did you trick us into going to her apartment so that she could take us prisoner?'

'No!' Ratsy cries. 'I was showing off to you, that was all . . . but Wackford found out.'

'So why didn't he lock you up with the rest of her workforce?' demands Wilhamina.

'Because Gretsch thought I might be kinda useful. I knew you and you knew about Animalia. I had to do what they said, guys . . . I had to. I'm not as tough . . . as strong-willed as you two –'

'And he *did* find out the password!' Froggo points out, stepping up behind them.

'I'm real sorry,' says Ratsy. 'Can you forgive me?'

Wilhamina puts a coat around his shivering

shoulders. 'I forgive you,' she says.

'Me too,' says Wirral. 'After all, you did save my life.'

'I did?'

Wirral nods. 'The car, remember? You pulled me out of the way of that car when I first set foot in Megatropolis.'

Now it's Ratsy's turn to grin. 'That's right! So I did!'

'And if they can forgive you, Ratsy, so can we!' booms Chief Bison. 'But, as for these two, they're a different matter.' He strides across the sand to Wackford and Gretsch, who are now tied together, back to back, with leafy vines. 'We'll have to think of a suitable punishment for you.'

Without her high-heeled shoes and wig, and with her fancy clothes dripping wet and ruined, Gretsch looks anything but threatening.

And Wackford? Without his whip, he looks like one defeated and seriously overweight rat.

As the animals take down the barricade and begin to get Animalia ready for the biggest celebration party in the island's history, Wirral, Wilhamina and Ratsy climb aboard the beached gunboat, with the aid of a friendly giraffe, called Jeffrey, who lets them use his neck as a gangplank.

'Show us how we can radio the guards' station in the main factory,' Wirral tells Ratsy.

'Why?' asks the rat.

'You'll see,' says Wilhamina.

Pleased to be able to help at last, Ratsy leads them to the bridge and presses a few buttons. 'Speak in there,' he says.

Wilhamina picks up the radio transmitter. 'This is Wilhamina calling Alfredo, Wilhamina calling Alfredo

. . . Do you receive me, Alfredo?'

A few moments later a tiny voice crackles across the airwaves: 'ALFREDO HERE. READING YOU LOUD AND CLEAR.'

'We've got the password!' says Wilhamina. 'It's INCARCERATE.'

There's a clickety-clack as Alfredo the flea jumps on each letter in turn: I-N-C-A-R-C-E-R-A-T-E. Then he jumps on 'Enter'.

Then? Silence, interrupted only by the crackle of static on the radio.

Finally, Alfredo speaks at last: 'IT WORKED!' He whoops with joy. 'I CAN OPEN ALL THE DOORS!'

'Then do it!' shouts Wirral. He, Wilhamina and Ratsy give each other a group hug.

'Great teamwork,' says Froggo from outside a porthole. 'Climb aboard, my furry friends. There's more to be done.'

*   *   *

Only a few days have passed but, in that time, a whole flotilla of boats has been assembled in the docks of Megatropolis. Each is crammed with as many of the freed animals as it can take. There's a rowing boat full of grubby bunnies, a canoe containing a young elephant at the back and a fox at the front, an old cargo ship with so many different types of creature it looks like a modern-day Noah's Ark – and that's just three vessels in hundreds. Smaller vessels are tied to bigger ones; those with engines will tow those without. Up in the air is the balloon, with Froggo, Wirral and Wilhamina looking down on the incredible scene beneath them.

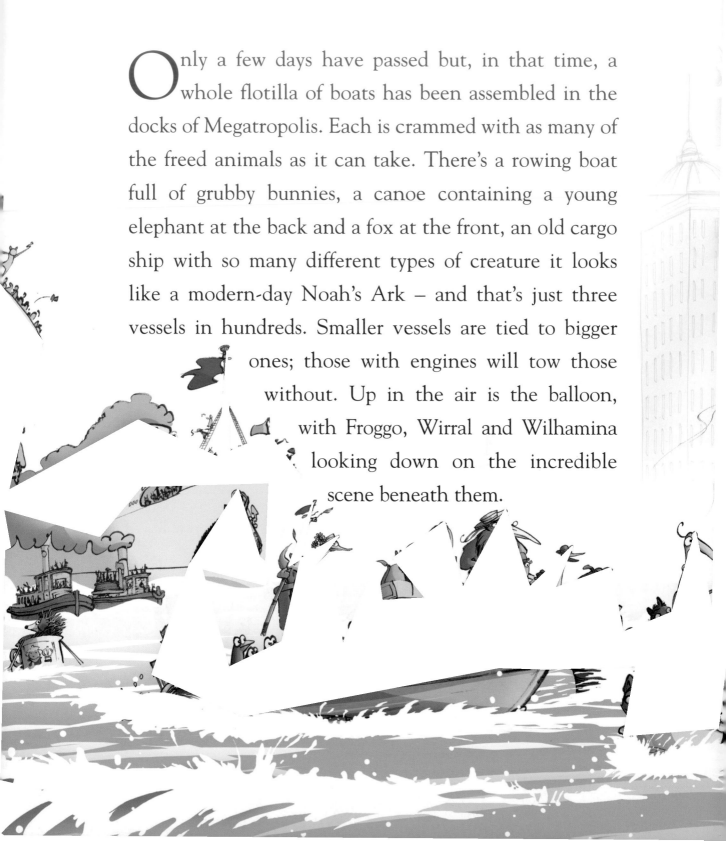

'Look, it's Gladys!' Wilhamina points.

Sure enough, far below, Gladys the toothless crocodile has swum out of a drainage pipe into the harbour, a group of happy sewer rats on her back . . . and they're all singing opera. She's the lead, of course, and they're the chorus.

'And there's Snooze!' says Wirral and, moments later, the owl comes in to land, perching on the edge of the basket. He looks at them through bleary eyes.

'It's a bit of an early start for me,' he yawns. 'But just to let you know that the Woodland creatures are all present and ready to depart. We've named our boat *Sugartail*, in honour of your mother, Wirral.' He blinks his great big eyes and clears his throat. 'Though why we couldn't set sail at night, I'll never know . . .'

'Then let's get going,' says Froggo. 'To Animalia!' he cries. On this signal, Wirral and Wilhamina fire flares into the air like giant fireworks. Ratsy, in a sea captain's hat, waves up at them from the lead boat. Engines start. Whistles blow. Horns blare. They're off to a new life!

* * *

The excitement that day is matched only by the excitement when the ragbag fleet finally reaches the island. It's arrival day at Animalia! Each animal is greeted individually, and the strong and the tall lift the weak and the small off the vessels.

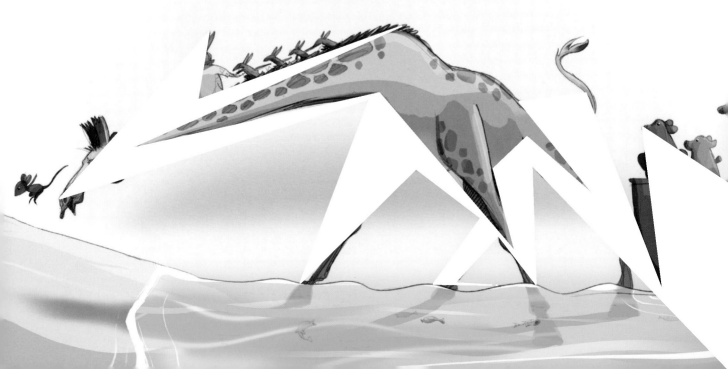

Once they're all ashore, the celebrations begin. Chief Bison makes a speech, interrupted time and time again by cheering from the islanders, old and new.

Then it's party time. It's time for the biggest tropic island hum in Animalia's history. Everyone rejoices.

Everyone, that is, except Wackford, who's now in a waiter's uniform (two sizes too small for him) carrying heaving trays of food to the animals he once frightened with his whip . . . and the very bald Gretsch, who's been made the official baby-sitter for the night. Muddles, the baby hippo, is circling her, feinting punches with his boxing gloves, while a young ostrich

and his friends are busy covering her in custard. Why? Because it's fun.

The band strikes up and, in one voice, the animals sing Animalia's anthem, *WE ALL STAND TOGETHER!*

Wirral turns to Wilhamina. 'If only Mum was with us,' he says. 'It's thanks to her and her stories that we're all here now.'

'She is here,' says Wilhamina.
There, painted in the night sky, is what
looks like a squirrel with a bushy tail,
powdery and white. Like sugar.

THE END
of the beginning

'You can judge a man's true character
by the way he treats his fellow animals.'

Snooze

Page 3

Black tailed godwit

CHAZU DUNN
CUSTOMER

Pencils for
page 4